How Do You Get A Mouse To Smile?

by
Bonnie Grubman

illustrated by
Cornelius Van Wright

Published in the United States of America by Star Bright Books, Inc., 30-19 48th Avenue, Long
Island City, NY 11101.

The name Star Bright Books and the Star Bright Books logo are registered trademarks of Star Bright
Books, Inc. Visit www.starbrightbooks.com. For bulk orders, email orders@starbrightbooks.com

Hardback ISBN-13: 978-1-59572-172-3
Paperback ISBN-13: 978-1-59572-167-9

Printed in China 9 8 7 6 5 4 3 2 1

Designed by Douglass V.M.R. Ridgeway

Library of Congress Cataloging-in-Publication Data

Grubman, Bonnie.
 How do you get a mouse to smile? / by Bonnie Grubman ; illustrated by Cornelius Van Wright.
 p. cm.
  Summary: Lyle goes to great lengths to entertain his furry friend.
  ISBN 978-1-59572-172-3 (hard back : alk. paper) --
  ISBN 978-1-59572-167-9 (paper back : alk. paper)
   [1. Stories in rhyme. 2. Mice--Fiction. 3. Pets--Fiction. 4. Smiling-- Fiction.
   5. Humorous stories.] I. Van Wright, Cornelius, ill. II. Title.
    PZ8.3.G91915Ho 2009
    [E]--dc21
      2009003445

For my precious husband, children, and
four-legged buddy. You give me infinite
reasons to smile every day.

–B.G.

A riddle, a diddle,
a riddle for Lyle.
How do you get
a mouse to smile?

Hmmmm . . .

You could whistle a **tune** with a mouthful of **gum**,

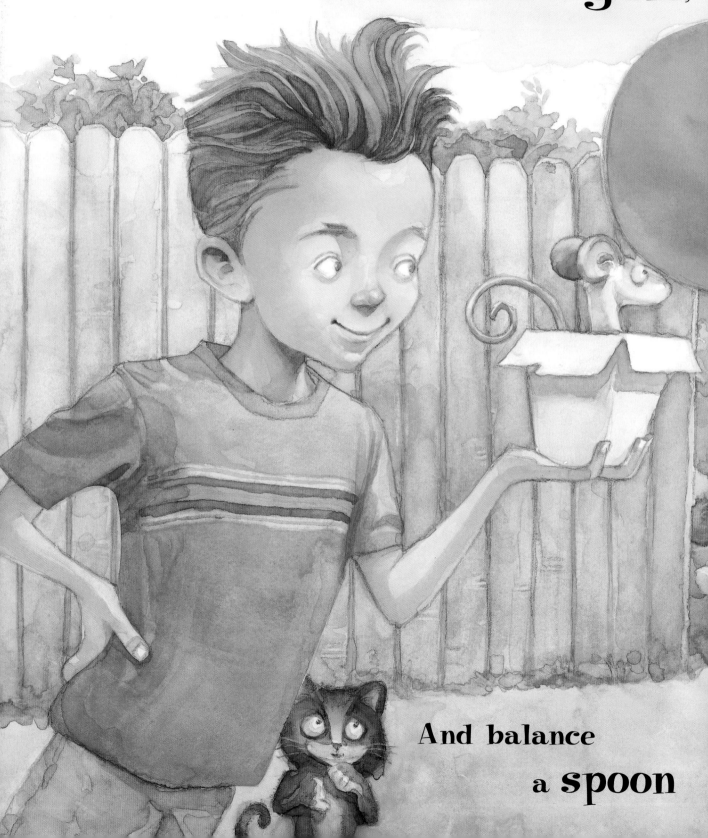

And balance **a spoon**

on the tip of
your **thumb**.

You could make silly faces and look like a goon,
And boogie and rock with a friendly baboon.

You could
stand on your head
and wrinkle your **nose**,
And say something funny
while holding a **pose**.

You could bark
and quack
and cluck
and moo...

These are some things
you could try to **do**
to get a mouse to smile.

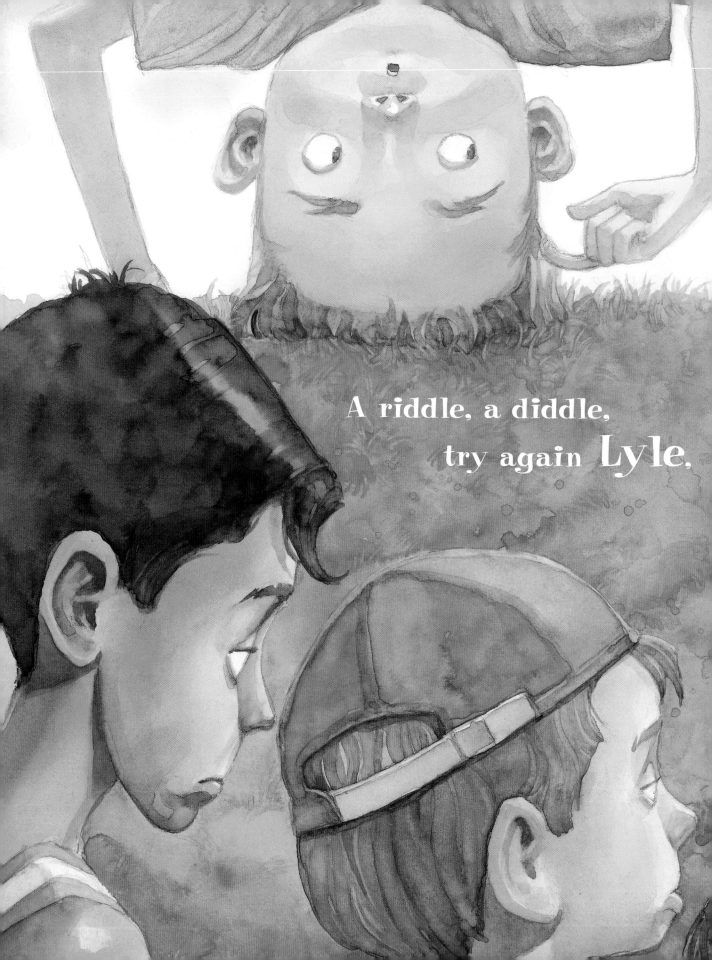

those things won't get a mouse to smile.

Then ...

You could really be goofy
        and walk like a **duck**,
And put your toe
        in the faucet
        and say that it's **stuck**.

You could stand on one elbow

and wink your left **eye**,

And pull out a plum

from Jack Horner's **pie**.

You could pretend to be clumsy and slip on a **peel**,
Or trip on your foot and make it look **real**.
You could roar like a lion and startle the **cat**.
No doubt in my mind it would smile at **that!**

You could make a rabbit
hop out of your
shoe....

These are some things
you could definitely **do**
to get a mouse to **smile.**

A riddle, a diddle,

so sorry Lyle,

that still won't get

a mouse to smile.

WELL THEN!

You could steady a plate on the tip of your **lip,**
while you juggle three balls
and do a **back-flip.**

You could hold on tight to a flying **trapeze,**

And make the mouse think you're going to sneeeeeze...

You could put on an act and pretend to **faint,**

And tumble backwards into a can of paint.

You could **slide**
upside down
a fireman's **pole**,
And land head first
in a goldfish **bowl.**

You could twist
        like a pretzel
and bellow and **shout**,
And huff and puff
        'til your lungs
                tucker **out**.
You could laugh
        'til you cry
                and fall flat
                    on the **floor**,

And howl
'til you're blue
and can't take
anymore.

There's only one way

to get a mouse to smile ...